Ruby Rogers
Tell Me About It

Ruby Rogers
Tell Me About It

Sue Limb

Illustrations by Bernice Lum

BLOOMSBURY

First published in Great Britain in 2008 by Bloomsbury Publishing Plc
36 Soho Square, London, WID 3QY

A CIP catalogue record of this book is available from the British Library

ISBN 978 0 7475 9246 4

All papers used by Bloomsbury Publishing are natural, recyclable
products made from wood grown in well-managed forests.
The manufacturing processes conform to the environmental
regulations of the country of origin.

Printed in Great Britain by Clays Ltd, St Ives Plc

1 3 5 7 9 10 8 6 4 2

www.suelimbbooks.co.uk
www.bloomsbury.com

CHAPTER 1

Stop bossing me about!

'THE WEATHER forecast is brilliant for once!' Mum was gabbling excitedly as Dad started the car. 'Oh, I do love this time of year! Whitsun's the start of the summer, really, isn't it? Ooh, look at those swallows! Bless their little hearts!' Mum has been almost illegally perky since she recovered from her op. It's great to see her so bubbly.

I was feeling pretty bubbly myself. A trip to the seaside! And this was kind of like sneaking an extra summer holiday in, because it was only the end of May and our main summer hol wouldn't be till August.

My monkeys were sharing the back seat with me, of course. There was heaps of room, because Joe wasn't coming with us. He was staying home 'revising for his A levels.' Huh! I know what that means. Watching TV for hours on end and going out to parties with the revolting Tiffany.

I suppose I should have been glad Joe wasn't coming, because it meant I wouldn't have to put up with the torment of constant teasing. But in a funny kind of way, I was sad instead.

'And don't worry about feeling lonely, Ruby,' said Mum, turning round and beaming at me. 'Because Sasha is just the same age as you – oh, I'll just send Deb a text to tell them we're on our way, shall I, Brian?'

'Yeah, go for it,' said Dad. 'I'd text them every five minutes if I were you. Tell them we're just going down Horsfield Road.'

'Shut up, Brian, don't be silly,' said Mum.

I began to go off into a daydream while Mum was texting. What was Quaymouth going to be like? I wondered if there would be an adventure playground with some ropes and platforms. That's the sort of thing I like.

'You'll love Sasha,' said Mum, after she'd sent her text off. 'She's ever such a nice girl. So polite. And guess what! She plays the violin! Plus she already speaks a bit of French – they learn it at St Joseph's.'

Though I was looking forward to meeting Sasha, the news that she played the violin came as a bit of a blow. And I hoped she wouldn't start talking French all over the place. St Joseph's is a rather posh school on the other side of town, so I'd never met Sasha, even though her mum, Deb, is one of Mum's friends at work.

Mum's phone rang. She's just got an ordinary beeping tone. She doesn't bother with any of those fancy ringtones. Mine is the Kaiser Chiefs singing 'RUBYRUBYRUBYRUBY', and Joe's is of chains being dragged about.

'Hello?' she said. 'Oh, Deb! . . . Yes, we've just left. We're just going past Tesco's. Isn't it nice not to have to buy groceries? . . . Yes, I'm sick to death of self-catering. I mean, self-catering's exactly what we have to do at home, isn't it? . . . OK, right, well, have a good journey. See you there! Bye!' She put her phone away and turned to Dad.

'They're already at Warminster!' she said. 'Almost halfway! Mind you, Paul's got a BMW.' I think a BMW is a very flash car. Sasha's dad is a businessman.

'You won't see many geography teachers with a BMW,' said Dad rather sourly. 'I can't help it if they're already at Warminster. You know this old bus won't do more than sixty without overheating.'

'Of course not!' cried Mum, laughing. 'It's not a *competition*, Brian. I wouldn't want to drive fast, anyway. I think it's stupid. I'm very happy to potter down there slowly.'

'Even if it means they'll have first pick of the rooms?' asked Dad slyly.

'Oh goodness, I never even thought of that!' cried Mum. 'It couldn't matter less. Who cares? I'm sure all the rooms are lovely, anyway.'

'Are we staying in a hotel?' I asked. It would be amazing to stay in one of those seaside hotels you see in old films. All the tables have white tablecloths, and there are palm trees dotted about and a young man with shiny hair is playing a grand piano while people eat cakes off silver cake stands and talk about the latest murder.

'No, love, we're staying at The Magpie Bed and Breakfast,' said Mum. 'The woman running it sounded very nice and friendly.'

'You'd be friendly if you thought people were going to come and pay you sixty quid a night just

to stay in one of your rooms,' said Dad.

'Brian! Don't be an idiot! I'd absolutely *hate* it if people came and stayed in our house for the night! I wouldn't do it even for £160!'

I started to daydream about Quaymouth. Mum had showed me a picture of the beach, covered with people.

'So what are you hoping to do, Ruby?' asked Mum.

'I want to make sandcastles,' I said. 'And go on walks in woods. And have fish and chips in a cafe. And go for a trip in a boat.'

'What about you, Brian?' she asked Dad.

'My secret plan is to lie in a deckchair for a week,' said Dad, 'with a handkerchief over my face, while fat women run past in bikinis. Like in the old postcards.'

'Oh, don't be awful!' said Mum. 'You'll want to go birdwatching, I expect – and I'm looking forward to seeing all those lovely old houses. It's where Jane Austen went on holiday, you know!' Mum had packed a load of old books. 'I'm just looking forward to reading for hours and hours – lying on the beach if the weather's warm enough.'

'If the weather's warm enough,' said Dad, 'my main plan is to teach Ruby to swim.'

I felt a bit nervous about this. I really wish I could swim. Yasmin and Froggo and Max can all swim. Lauren and Hannah go swimming together all the time. But I've always preferred paddling. I can't work out how to wade in deep and let go. It's slightly frightening. If Dad could manage to teach me to swim, that would be brilliant. But I had a secret fear that somehow, I would never be able to do it.

'And if the weather's bad, there's a lovely spa,' said Mum. 'I'm thinking of having a day there anyway, and a massage and everything, just to pamper myself.'

'Don't try to drag me there,' groaned Dad. 'There's nothing I hate more than being pampered.'

After a while Mum switched the car radio on, and I stared out of the window at the countryside. It looked very beautiful. All the trees had their new leaves on, and the gardens were full of flowers. There were several woods, and I pointed them out to the monkeys, and we decided we were on an expedition to find an ancient temple in the rainforest, and I started to get excited by the idea.

The ruined temple was covered by creepers, overgrown, with strange spooky shadowy arches and dripping stones . . . this was an adventure that could last all week.

'OK guys,' said Stinker (he's boss). 'First we gotta make sure no other gang's moved into the temple and is hidin' out there. We need a scout to go and do a recce.'

'I'll be a scout!' said Funky. 'I'll do a recce!' He's quite bendy, so he would easily be able to wriggle through the branches of the trees.

'What can I do?' asked Hewitt, my third and newest monkey. He has a tennis racket permanently fastened to his arm, so really his life has to revolve around sport.

'You keep close to me,' growled Stinker, 'and if

there's any trouble wid bad guys there, you're gonna whip their tails wid your racket!'

We hadn't got very far with this plan when suddenly the car stopped and we piled out.

'Here we are!' said Mum excitedly. Apparently we had arrived in Quaymouth. I'd been trekking in the jungle for hours, so I had lost all track of time. We were in a small car park behind a big house. Mum and Dad got out of the car and yawned and stretched rather stiffly. I jumped out, and gathered up the monkeys.

'There's Paul and Deb's car,' said Mum. 'Let's go and say hello first. Leave the cases where they are, and lock the car, Brian.'

'Stop bossing me about,' said Dad. 'I'm not an idiot.' He locked the car. 'On second thoughts,' he went on, 'OK. I admit I am an idiot, but please stop bossing me about anyway.'

We went round to the front door and rang the bell. The door opened almost immediately. A woman with very thick glasses stood there. Her eyes looked a bit frightening, magnified and huge. But she was very jolly.

'Ah!' she beamed. 'Welcome to Magpie House! I'm Maria Trescothick. It must be Mrs and Mrs Rogers and – what's your name again, dear?'

'Ruby,' I said.

'Ruby! How nice! What lovely names girls have these days, don't they? Ruby and Sasha! Well, do come in – I'll show you to your room.'

We went inside and followed Mrs Trescothick upstairs. One door we passed was open, and inside was a girl about my age sitting in the window seat looking out across the beach.

'There's Sasha!' said Mrs Trescothick. Then Sasha's mum, Deb, appeared, and she and Mum had a big reunion thing.

'Ruby, this is Sasha,' said Deb. 'Sasha, come and say hello to Ruby!' Sasha got up off the window seat and came towards me. She was taller than me and had long blonde crinkly hair, done up in a pony tail. Yasmin would have loved her hair. Her eyes were big and blue. She smiled at me.

'Hi, Ruby,' she said.

'Hi, Sasha,' I replied. There was an embarrassed pause.

'Well, we must go and see our room,' said Mum. 'We don't want to hold Mrs Trescothick up . . .'

'Call me Maria, please!' laughed Mrs Trescothick. 'Everybody does. Here's your room – just across from Deb and Paul!' She threw open the door and we went in.

'Lovely!' said Mum. 'What fabulous curtains!'

But anyone could see that though Sasha's family had a big sunshiny yellow room that overlooked the seafront, ours was a grey room at the back that overlooked the car park.

CHAPTER 2

That would be lovely, wouldn't it, Ruby?

'IT'S LOVELY!' said Mum. 'What pretty curtains! And tea-making facilities! That's handy!' There was a big double bed for Mum and Dad, and a little bed in the corner for me.

'The en suite's through here,' said Maria, opening a door. Mum peeped through to the bathroom.

'Oh, fabulous!' she said. 'A proper bath as well! Lovely!'

'Anything you want, just come downstairs and ring the little bell in the hall,' said Maria. Her eyes flashed hugely behind her thick glasses.

'Thanks ever so much!' said Mum. 'Bring the cases up, Brian, and I'll make a cup of tea.'

'Oh, I'll be serving tea for you downstairs in the lounge in a couple of minutes,' said Maria. 'And home-baked cakes. We always offer tea for our guests on arrival. Your friends will be down there too.'

Five minutes later we were all sitting in the lounge. It was at the front and there was a huge window with amazing views of the sea. I couldn't wait to get out on to the beach. But Maria's chocolate cake smelt wonderful, so I didn't mind sitting in here for a few minutes first.

Sasha's mum, Deb, was talking, while my mum poured the tea. Deb has straggly blonde hair and a big gap between her front teeth. She laughs a lot, and sometimes, when she's getting carried away with an idea, a little bit of spit flies out of her mouth, but you have to pretend you don't notice.

'We stopped for lunch on the way down in this *weird* little pub!' Deb was saying. 'Miles from nowhere, and the man looked just like a gorilla! And he came and served us in his vest! Didn't he, Paul?'

'It was a singlet,' said Sasha's dad. 'Yes. The King's Arms, Draycombe. Definitely a place to avoid. It was just off the B404. I hope you didn't

make the mistake of going down the A3078?' He looked at my dad.

'Yes, I'm afraid we did make that mistake,' said Dad. 'Got held up.'

'Roadworks,' said Sasha's dad, removing his base-ball cap and scratching his head. He didn't have much hair, and what he did have was shaved. He was quite fat, and wearing shorts. From where I was sitting, I had to look straight at his fat hairy knees. Luckily Maria had given me a delicious chocolate cake and some juice, so I tried to con-centrate on that.

'You get regular traffic updates on Radio Five Live,' said Paul importantly. 'So we knew we had to avoid the A3078. Plus we've got Sat Nav. Have you got Sat Nav, Brian?'

'No,' said Dad. 'But I have got Lav Nav. It tells me where the nearest toilets are.' Everybody laughed, except Paul.

'Oh, you are a one, Brian!' shrieked Deb.

'He got that joke out of his magazine,' said Mum.

'What they ought to do here,' said Paul, stirring his tea, 'is build a marina. Round the other side, where the harbour is.'

'Oh, no, Paul, that would spoil it!' said Deb. 'It's

such a pretty little harbour! We went for a walk the moment we arrived, didn't we, Sasha?'

Sasha nodded. She was eating a cake with pink icing on. It was decorated with silver balls. Sasha was picking off the silver balls and leaving them on her plate.

'Maybe after tea Sasha can show Ruby where the harbour is?' Deb went on, smiling at me.

I tried to look grateful, but really I just wanted to run off on to the beach by myself. I didn't want anybody to show me things. I wanted to find out for myself. I'd finished my cake and juice now, and I kept looking out of the window at the amazing beach.

'That's where the money is,' said Paul. 'Marinas. Get the jet set in with their yachts. Take this place upmarket. That's what I'd do.' He sipped his tea and shook his head thoughtfully as if he felt really sorry for Quaymouth having to muddle on without him.

'There's a wonderful view of the harbour,' said Deb. 'We saw a couple of old ladies walking along the quayside, and they looked just like a couple of penguins, didn't they, Sasha? Ha ha ha!' She spat right into the milk jug. Thank goodness we'd more or less finished our tea.

'Didn't they, love?' Deb went on. Sasha nodded. She'd finished her cake, but left all the silver balls. She saw me looking at them.

'I don't eat silver balls,' she said to me, tossing her head kind of defiantly. 'They've got chemicals in.'

'Sasha was thinking of doing a drawing of the harbour, maybe, weren't you, pet?' Deb went on. Sasha nodded. 'It's for the school art competition. She came second with one of her drawings, last year.'

'It was a *painting*,' said Sasha. 'Not a drawing.'

'That's right! We had it framed, and it's hanging in our sitting room. You must come and see it one day, Ruby!' I tore my eyes away from the beach for a minute and tried to look interested.

'That would be lovely, wouldn't it, Ruby?' said Mum, glaring slightly at me.

'Yes,' I said politely, even though I was starting to want to scream.

'I hear you're a bit of a birdwatcher, Brian,' said Paul, finishing his tea and smacking his lips. 'I suppose you're planning to take a look at Fingleton Reserve?'

'He certainly is!' said Mum. 'I packed his binoculars!'

'There won't be much of interest there at this time of year,' said Paul, sounding rather satisfied. 'Although you might be lucky enough to see a bearded tit.'

Deb burst into gales of loud laughter and a little bit of spit soared out of her mouth and landed on her husband's knee. Well, at least they were keeping it in the family. Her husband gave her a dirty look and wiped it off with his hand.

'Are you a member of the RSPB, Brian?' Paul asked.

'Yes,' said Dad. 'But when it comes to birdwatching, I'm a bit of a beginner.'

'Ruby's got a way with birds,' said Mum. Suddenly everybody looked at me. I felt hot. 'There's this little family of robins in our garden, and she's training them to eat out of her hand.' I wished Mum would leave me out of it. It seemed as if the mums were having a Wonderful Daughters Boasting Competition.

'How lovely, Ruby!' said Deb.

'It's shocking about the northern bald ibis, isn't it?' sighed Paul, shaking his head and tut-tutting. I wondered what on earth he was talking about. Presumably some kind of bird.

'Is it?' said Dad. 'I'm afraid I'm not up to speed on ibises.'

'Really?' said Paul, looking surprised. 'I would have thought being a geography teacher you'd have heard about this project in Syria.'

'OK, I confess,' said Dad. 'Although I am a geography teacher, I'm not a hundred per cent sure where Syria is. I mean, I couldn't find it in the dark, say, in a power cut.' Everybody except Paul laughed. I felt proud of Dad. He was way more cool than Sasha's dad, who was just boasting all the time.

'What is this project in Syria?' asked Mum. I wished she hadn't asked. I was longing so desperately to get out on to the beach, it actually hurt. The sand was dazzling. Lucky people were running to and fro, flying kites, paddling, swimming. Seagulls were swooping and calling: beach balls were whizzing through the air. All this was happening out on the wonderful beach behind Paul's head.

'In Syria,' said Paul, 'they've fitted these ibises with satellite transmitters to try and find out where they migrate to for the winter. They're endangered.'

'Oh! How cruel!' exclaimed Deb, spitting on a potted plant on the coffee table.

'It's not cruel,' said Paul slowly, as if he was talking to an idiot. Well, he'd been married to Deb for years, so he should know. But even if she was an idiot, I still thought she was heaps nicer than him. 'They don't interfere with the birds flying or anything. If they can find out where they overwinter, it'll help conservation measures.'

I was now almost bursting with the desire to escape. Conversation about conservation was more than I could take.

'I'd like to fit you with a satellite transmitter, Paul!' laughed Deb. 'I'd like to see where you spend some of your lunch hours! Ha ha! ha!'

I couldn't bear it any longer. I jumped to my feet. Everybody looked a bit startled.

'Please may I go out on the beach?' I asked.

'Oh, yes, of course, love,' said Mum. 'But don't talk to any —'

She was cut short by Dad jumping up as well. He kicked the coffee table slightly and everything sort of rocked a bit, but nothing fell over or broke.

'It's OK,' said Dad. 'I'll go with Ruby.' He grabbed my hand.

'Oh, no, you don't, Brian!' said Mum with a playful grin. 'You jolly well stay here and help me unpack. Then we can both go out on the beach, all right? Maybe Sasha and Ruby would like to go out together first?'

Sasha stood up and straightened her ponytail. My heart sank. She held out her hand to me and smiled.

'Come on, Ruby,' she said. 'I'll look after you.'

CHAPTER 3
Stop acting like an idiot!

I KIND OF slithered past her like a snake and raced out of doors. Sasha followed me.

'Ruby!' I heard her shout. 'Wait for me!' I raced on down some steps on to the beach. There was wind in my face. It was fantastic. I kicked off my flip-flops and ran down to the edge of the sea. Toddlers were paddling. Little kids were playing football. 'Ruby! Wait!' I tiptoed into the sea. It was freezing! I squealed, but it was nice too.

'Ruby, what are you doing? You haven't got a towel!' Sasha had arrived now, and she was standing there on the sand, with her hands on her hips.

'Who cares?' I grinned, bending down and scooping up handfuls of water and throwing it about. I wouldn't say I was actually trying to hit her in the eye, not actually *trying*, but sometimes these things happen by accident.

'Ruby! Stop it!' She backed off a bit, looking cross. 'Calm down! Stop acting like an idiot!' A dog ran up behind her.

'Watch out!' I shouted. 'There's a dog behind you!' I kind of hoped it might knock her over. Sasha turned round. She didn't look a bit scared. She held her hand out to the dog.

'Come here!' she called. 'Come! Good boy! Good boy! Aren't you a lovely dog, then?' She stroked his head. Then he ran off.

I paddled to the shore. Sasha turned to me. 'I love dogs,' she said. 'I'm not frightened of them. We've got a couple of black Labradors called Jet and Harry. Have you got any dogs?'

'No,' I said. 'Because Mum and Dad both go out to work. We think it's cruel to keep dogs shut in all day.'

'Ours aren't shut in all day!' replied Sasha, quick as a flash and slightly stressy. 'My granny looks after them. She lives just down the road. She takes them for walks, everything. She used to be a dog breeder. She won prizes at Crufts for her mastiffs.' I couldn't compete on this subject, so I didn't say anything.

We started to walk along the beach. It went on and on. The bay was huge. The waves were sparkling, but not dangerously high or rough. It was a brilliant place.

'Isn't it lovely here?' I sighed.

'It's OK. But last year we went to Lanzarote,' said Sasha.

'Where?' I'd never heard of Lanzarote.

'It's in the Canaries,' said Sasha. I was puzzled. I wondered if it had something to do with birds again.

'Is that . . . because your Dad likes birds?' I asked. Sasha frowned and stared at me.

'It's just called the Canary Islands,' she said. 'It's ever so warm and there are palm trees everywhere. We rented a villa with its own pool.'

'Nice,' I said.

'Have you ever been abroad?' asked Sasha.

'We went to France once,' I said. 'Camping.'

'Oh,' said Sasha, sounding rather disappointed. She didn't ask me anything about our camping trip. We walked on, past some people who were

making a huge, brilliant sandcastle.

'Shall we make a sandcastle?' I asked. I had a sudden idea for a big square castle with four turrets and a moat around it – and when the tide came in, the moat could fill with water.

'No,' said Sasha. 'I don't want to get my clothes dirty.' I was amazed. Who cares if clothes get dirty? I mean, that's what they're for, isn't it?

'Why don't you go back and change?' I suggested, hoping she might disappear for a bit and leave me on my own to make my own sandcastle privately.

'No,' she said. 'I can change later.' She went on walking. I was slightly tempted to run away, but somehow I managed to stay by her side.

'Who's your best friend at school?' she asked.

'Yasmin,' I said. I had to remember to send Yasmin a postcard. Although I would obviously text her loads, too. And no prizes for what the next text would be about. My weird new companion.

'*Jasmine*, you mean,' said Sasha.

'What?' I was puzzled.

'It's Jasmine, not Yasmin,' said Sasha.

'No it's not!' I snapped. How dare she tell me how to pronounce my own best friend's name? 'It's *Yasmin*! She's Turkish.'

'Your best friend is *Turkish*?' Sasha looked surprised. 'Can she speak English?'

'Of course she can speak English!' I shouted. 'She *is* English!'

'You just said she was Turkish.'

'She's English and Turkish. Her family is Turkish. Her granny still lives in Turkland. I mean, Turkey.' I was really annoyed with myself for that little slip. It's hard to put a bighead in her place if stupid things like *Turkland* are coming out of your mouth.

'My best friend is called Charlotte,' said Sasha. 'She goes skiing and her granny lives in Provence.' I didn't know where Provence was, but it sounded posh.

I was really majorly fed up with Sasha. Everything seemed like a competition to her. I decided to stop trying to compete and, instead, secretly take the mickey.

'My granny is really, really poor,' I said. 'She lives in a shed with a donkey and she gets her food out of the waste bins outside the burger bar.'

Sasha gave me a funny look.

'There's no need to be stupid,' she said with her lips kind of tight like a head teacher. She was wrong, though. There certainly *was* a need to be stupid. I had to try and break the evil spell we seemed to be under. Yasmin would have laughed. But I hadn't actually seen Sasha laugh yet.

She stopped and looked back. 'See how far we've come,' she said. 'It must be at least two miles.'

'Don't be an idiot! It's only a few hundred metres!' I grinned. 'You can see the B&B. In fact, I think that's your dad coming down the steps.'

'Don't call me an idiot,' said Sasha coldly. 'You're the one who's an idiot. At least I didn't bring any cuddly toys. How old are you, for goodness' sake?'

'They're not cuddly toys,' I protested. 'They're my monkeys. I'm going to study monkeys when I'm grown up. I'm going to go to Costa Rica to see the howler monkeys. Name a monkey, and I'll tell you about it!' It was a kind of challenge.

Sasha looked at me as if I was from another planet. She shook her head and sighed.

'Ruby, I'm sorry, but I really don't want to know about any monkeys right now!'

I was disappointed. It had been a chance to score a few points. I bet she knew nothing about monkeys. But at least she had called me Ruby and said she was sorry. It would be awful if we started this holiday as enemies.

'I'm sorry I called you an idiot,' I said. 'I don't mean it really. I call Yasmin an idiot all the time.' Sasha looked down at the sand and smoothed her skirt thoughtfully. But she didn't say she was sorry for calling me an idiot. Instead, she looked up suddenly, right into my eyes.

'OK,' she said. 'Now, you're going to be a castaway on a desert island, and I'm going to be the pirate chief who captures you. You'll be my slave.'

CHAPTER 4
Isn't she a lovely girl?

A T THIS POINT I really did run away, fast, back towards the B&B. I twisted and turned and dodged and skipped past all the people. I knew I could run faster than Sasha because she was tall and her legs were more wobbly than mine. And I don't suppose she would run very fast anyway in case it damaged her clothes.

As I ran, I saw Mum and Dad coming down the steps of the B&B and on to the beach. I saw Mum bend down and pick something up. Whoops! It must have been my flip-flops. I'd kicked them off as soon as I got on the sand. I saw Dad scanning the beach, looking for me. He waved. I waved back. I'd be with him in a minute. Bliss!

A few moments later I jumped into Dad's arms and he whirled me round and round and round. We don't do that very much at home, partly because there isn't enough room and partly because he's usually tired out from being a geography teacher.

'Be careful of your back, Brian!' said Mum. Dad finished the whirling and let go of me.

'My back is fine!' said Dad. 'The best thing for my back is swimming. So this week is going to sort it out.'

Sasha arrived, puffing. I put my arm round Dad. I was keen to avoid becoming Sasha's slave. She couldn't kidnap me if I was actually attached to my dad, could she?

'Did you have a lovely walk, girls?' said Mum.

'Yes, thanks!' said Sasha. 'It was brilliant. Ruby made me laugh. She's so funny.'

Mum looked pleased and proud, but I was amazed. I thought Sasha was going to complain about me.

'I'm just going in to get my shorts on, and see

what Mum's doing,' said Sasha, and she ran off towards the B&B.

'Isn't she a lovely girl?' said Mum. 'I'm so glad you're going to have somebody to play with, Ruby.'

I said nothing. I looked at the sand. There was a plastic bottle lying there that somebody had thrown away. It spoilt the beautiful soft sand to have litter lying about.

'Ruby?' said Mum. I looked up at her. She had a special expression on her face which appears when she suspects me of something. 'I said, Sasha's a lovely girl, isn't she?'

I knew there would be big trouble if I told them exactly what I thought of Sasha. I didn't want to spoil the mood by telling them what she was really like. Maybe I'd made a mistake, anyway. She'd seemed so nice just now, saying I was funny and stuff.

'She's OK,' I said. Mum and Dad exchanged a look.

'I expect you're missing Yasmin,' said Mum. 'Never mind. Remember when you first got to know Lauren, it was a while before you realised what a nice girl she was. It takes time to get to know somebody.'

I kicked a bit of sand about. Lauren had never been like Sasha: bossy and cocky. Lauren had just been shy.

'Never mind all this girly stuff about relationships!' said Dad. 'I'm going for a paddle! Coming, Ruby?' He grabbed my hand and we went off, laughing and splashing along the edge of the sea. We had such a good time. I forgot all about Sasha.

'Tomorrow,' said Dad, 'apparently it's going to be a lot warmer. Hot, in fact. Blame global warming, but at least we'll be able to swim. I'm going to teach you to swim whether you like it or not, Miss Rogers!'

I didn't see Sasha again until the evening meal. She'd changed into a blue dress with butterflies on it. It made her eyes look very, very blue. I was still wearing my shorts and T-shirt. Maria didn't seem to mind. She brought us steaming plates of tomato soup – my favourite.

'Did you have a nice afternoon?' she asked, her huge eyes goggling at us through her thick glasses.

'Ooooh, yes, lovely, thanks!' gushed Deb. Everything was always terrific with Deb. I really liked her, despite the spitting. 'Ruby and Sasha went for a walk on the beach, then Sasha and I went round to the harbour again and did some sketching.'

'And what do you think of our golf course, Paul?' asked Maria. Sasha's dad rubbed his bald head and looked thoughtful.

'I've seen worse,' he said. I cringed. Surely he should have said, *'Your golf course is fantastic'*? It sounded so rude. 'There's a fantastic golf course in Lanzarote, Brian,' he went on, turning to Dad. Dad looked a bit edgy, because basically he's bored stiff by golf and probably Lanzarote too. 'It's at the foot of this volcano, and there are palm trees everywhere, and cactuses, and lava. You'd love it, Brian, what with being a geography teacher and everything.'

I was afraid Maria would be hurt because he hadn't said anything nice about Quaymouth golf course, but she just bustled off to see to something in the kitchen.

'Of course,' said Dad, 'as a geography teacher, I am interested in lava, but I do like to keep it out of the bedroom if possible.' Everybody laughed except Paul. He didn't seem to hear jokes – maybe because he didn't listen to what anybody else said.

'Paul's not one for volcanic activity in the bedroom either! Ha ha!' said Deb. 'It's more like the Sahara desert when we switch the light out!' She did a kind of giggling scream. Though I liked her, I wished she wouldn't make rude grown-up type jokes in such a loud voice.

'Lovely soup, isn't it?' said Mum, trying to get the conversation back on to polite subjects. 'Home made.'

'I don't like it,' said Sasha quietly to her mum.

'Just leave it then, pet, it's all right,' whispered Deb. I ate all my soup and licked my lips to show that, when it came to tomato soup, I won hands down.

After the soup we had roast chicken with roast potatoes, carrots and peas. It was scrumptious, although I noticed Sasha left her carrots and peas.

'So, Sasha, do you want to be an artist when you grow up?' asked Mum.

'I want to do graphic design,' said Sasha. My brain reeled. What in the world was graphic design? Sasha sounded like somebody talking on the TV – an expert.

'She's always loved drawing,' said Deb, beaming at Sasha. 'Even when she was a toddler. Once – she was only about eighteen months old – I gave her some paper and a crayon, and she drew this dog, I mean, you could tell it was a dog, and when I told the doctor, she said, *Well, she must be very bright indeed if she's drawing something recognisable at eighteen months.*'

'Wow!' said Dad. 'Brilliant! Ruby still can't draw anything recognisable. If she tried to draw a dog, you'd probably think it was a fridge!' I felt furious and embarrassed. I liked it when Dad jokes and refuses to join in competitive boasting games, but he shouldn't make fun of me in front of other people. Especially *her*.

'Brian, don't be horrid!' said Mum. 'Art isn't Ruby's strong point, that's all. She's going to be a zoologist.' She said this with a kind of flourish. You could see she was trying to compete with Deb just a little bit. In fact, Mum still probably hadn't

quite recovered from hearing Sasha say she was going to be a graphic designer. It had been a scary moment, somehow.

'A zoologist! How lovely, Ruby!' said Deb. 'What's your favourite animal? – Oh, silly me! Of course, monkeys! You're famous for them. OK, then, what's your favourite monkey?' She was smiling at me but I felt she was treating me like a baby. Deb was asking me an extra-easy question just so I could say *something* instead of lurking shyly on the edge of things like a loser, while Sasha described her brilliant career as a thingummyjig.

'I don't have a favourite monkey,' I said icily. 'And I might not be a zoologist, anyway,' I directed this put-down at Mum.

'Have you had a better idea?' asked Mum, smiling encouragingly and no doubt hoping my new chosen career had very long words in it. I popped the last bit of roast potato in my mouth and started chewing it. Everybody was looking at me and waiting for my answer.

'Yes, Ruby!' said Deb, filling the pause with an encouraging smile. 'How are you planning to earn your living?' I swallowed the potato.

'By making sandcastles,' I said. I'd meant it to be kind of sulky and grumpy, but Mum and Dad and Deb roared with laughter and Sasha gave me a kind of evil look, as if she thought I'd ruined her moment of triumph. Tomorrow I would have to watch out.

CHAPTER 5
I don't like it!
I want to get out!

AS DAD TUCKED me in that night, he
whispered, 'That was a great gag about building sandcastles, Ruby! You're my hero!' Then he
kissed my head, winked and grinned and left me
to fall asleep with my monkeys.

'Dad is on my side,' I whispered to Stinker,
Funky and Hewitt. 'Basically, I think he hates
Sasha's dad as much as I hate Sasha.'

'Why are we on holiday with these people?'
asked Funky. 'You told us she wasn't interested in

monkeys! What sort of a person could say that? It's so hurtful!'

'Her mum Deb is Mum's friend at work,' I explained. 'Deb's ever so nice. Although she does say rude things loudly in public.'

'Thass the kind of dame I like!' growled Stinker in his gangster voice. 'Sassy!' I'm not sure what sassy means, exactly, but I could see why it might suit Deb. 'Enough of da girl talk!' Stinker went on. 'Less get back to da jungle!' I closed my eyes, and within moments I was somewhere else.

Next morning at breakfast, Maria-with-the-big-eyes asked us what our plans were.

'Shopping!' grinned Deb. 'Rhiannon and I are going to indulge in a few little luxuries! Handmade chocolates and maybe a quick peep in the lingerie shop! Not that Paul would notice! Ha ha ha!' I cringed over my cornflakes.

'Yes, and there might be some local craft stalls, too,' said Mum hastily. 'I'd love to get a special teapot or a vase or something.'

'Fancy a round of golf, Brian?' said Paul.

'No, thanks!' said Dad. 'I don't play, I'm afraid. Plus I have a very important project: teaching Ruby to swim.'

Sasha gave me a hard look. You could see she

42

was astonished that I couldn't swim, and that she regularly swam across the Atlantic to New York for the weekend.

'What about you, Sasha?' said Maria-with-the-big-eyes.

'I'll go shopping with Mum,' said Sasha. 'I want to go to the bookshop.'

'She's always got her nose in a book!' laughed Deb. This was another boast disguised as a joke.

'Yes, and some of the books she reads are the size of bricks!' said Paul. Of course, it would have to be big thick books that impressed him. After all, he was big and thick himself.

'That pub on the corner's got a plasma TV, Brian,' he said, turning to Dad. 'I thought maybe we could check out the motor racing this after-noon.'

'Sure,' said Dad. 'Great idea!' Mum and I secret-ly knew that Dad hates motor racing. Just the sound of the cars all roaring round the track makes him switch the TV off and run out into the garden. He really likes gardening and walking and birds and stuff.

But he couldn't admit he hated Formula One so soon after saying he couldn't play golf. It's a kind of game men play. So now poor Dad was going to have to go off to a crowded, noisy pub and watch fast cars screeching round a circuit all afternoon. I knew it would give him a headache.

I caught his eye briefly, and there was a moment of complete understanding. I knew just how he felt, and he knew that I knew, and was grateful. So far I had escaped having to plan something with Sasha. I was hoping my swimming lesson might last all day, then Dad and I would never have to spend any time with Paul and Sasha at all.

'And maybe Ruby and Sasha could go for a walk this afternoon, again,' said Mum. 'Or build one of your famous sandcastles, Ruby?' I almost kicked Mum under the table for ruining everything. But instead I had to smile and nod and say yes.

'Right!' said Dad. 'The swimming lesson calls! Excuse me! Come on, Ruby!' We'd all finished our breakfasts so it was time to go.

We spent a bit of time first up in our room, writing postcards to the grandparents and various friends. This was mainly because Mum said we mustn't go swimming straight after breakfast. We have to do what she says because she's a trained nurse. But once she'd gone off for her shopping trip with Deb, Dad and I decided our breakfasts

were now ancient history, and the moment had come to run into the sea.

We didn't run, actually, because it was quite cold. I had my water wings on and held on tight to Dad's hand.

'The trick is to go in slowly,' said Dad. 'Just splash around a bit and get used to the temperature of the water . . . Aaaaaargh!'

The freezing water came up to my knees, my thighs . . . I was dreading the moment when the waves would crash into my tummy.

'Ow! Brrrr!' That was the dreaded moment. But at least my legs and feet had got used to the cold water and it felt OK.

'Come on,' said Dad. 'Let's jump as each wave comes in.'

We did that for a bit, and as each wave came in, Dad lifted me up, and we laughed a lot, and it was fun.

'Right,' said Dad. 'Now you're nice and relaxed, let's go in a bit deeper.'

'But it's already up to my waist!' I said. 'It's all right for you: you're still paddling.'

'Come on, Ruby, don't be a wuss,' said Dad, smiling. 'Trust me. I'll carry you if you like.'

'Yes,' I said, and I sort of jumped up on to Dad and clung on like a monkey. He waded out into deeper water. I held on tight.

'You must trust me,' he said. 'Nothing bad will happen. You've got your water wings on, anyway, so it's literally impossible for you to go under.'

At this moment, out of the blue, a big wave hit me smack in the face. For a second, my nose, ears and eyes were full of salty, stinging water. I gasped and choked. I panicked. I coughed. I was almost sick.

'Steady on!' said Dad. 'It's all right. 'Relax! It was only a wave!'

'I want to get out!' I yelled. 'I don't like it! I want to get out!'

'Don't give up, Ruby,' said Dad. 'Come on, be a sport.'

'I hate it!' I yelled, coughing and spluttering. 'I want to get out! Take me back to the beach!' And I was in such a rage, I started to cry.

Dad was being so horrid. He'd said he'd look after me, that nothing bad could happen and to trust him. And then he'd let a nasty big wave smash into my face!

'OK, OK, calm down,' he said, sounding stressy. 'We'll get out if that's what you want.'

He carried me back to the beach. I was still coughing and choking. I had swallowed most of the sea. I had breathed in some of it. I was still slightly tempted to collapse dramatically on the sand and pretend to faint, just to pay him back for not looking after me properly.

As soon as we reached the sand, he put me down and wrapped me in a towel. I was still crying and coughing and in a terrible state.

'Calm down, Ruby, for God's sake,' said Dad. 'It's not the end of the world. Everybody's looking.'

'I don't care!' I snapped. I so hated Dad for making this happen to me. I started to shiver, but kind of madly, not because I was cold (although I was –

freezing), but because I was so upset. And then I heard a voice.

'Are you OK, Ruby?' I looked round. There was Sasha, staring at me, with her dad.

'Swallowed a bit of seawater, have you?' said her dad. And he was grinning – *grinning*! 'Don't worry, you'll live.' Then he winked at Dad. 'I always say, you can't beat a swimming pool for teaching kids to swim. You never know where you are with the sea.'

What a put-down! Although I hated Dad deeply at this moment, I hated Sasha's dad even more.

'So golf's off, is it?' said Dad, trying to sound superior even though he was clearly losing the battle for male supremacy.

'Oh, yes. I soon got given my orders by She Who Must Be Obeyed,' said Paul. 'Sasha decided against the shopping trip after all, so I'm on babysitting duty.'

'I'm not a baby!' said Sasha sharply. Her dad ignored her.

'But tell you what, Brian,' he went on, 'if you and Ruby are going to be here anyway, maybe Sasha could stay with you? Build a sandcastle, eh, Ruby?'

I shivered, and my teeth chattered madly as if to show how near death I was, and how building a sandcastle, especially with Sasha, might just push me over the edge.

'Sure,' said Dad. 'No problem. It would be a pleasure.'

CHAPTER 6

Oh dear, you poor thing!

SASHA PRODUCED a small spade, knelt down on the sand and started to dig. She looked up at me.

'You can help me with my sandcastle if you like, Ruby,' she said.

'In a minute,' I said, still shivering. 'I think I'm going to go in and change into some dry clothes, Dad. And maybe have a shower.'

'Good idea!' Dad hesitated. Paul had already walked off, dumping Sasha on us. 'Do you need help or can you manage?' This was a coded way of asking me if I wanted Sasha to come up to our room.

'I can manage,' I said. I ran back to the B&B, fuming. Holidays were supposed to be wonderful. This morning had been hellish, so far. My dad had nearly drowned me. Then Paul and Sasha had appeared. Then Sasha had invited me to 'help' with 'her' sandcastle. I vowed there and then that if I ever managed to get around to building a sand-castle this week, it was going to be mine, all mine.

Maria met me in the hall. Her huge eyes flared even larger when she saw me.

'Ruby!' she said. 'How did the swimming lesson go?'

'Awful,' I said. 'A huge wave hit me in the face.' I coughed a bit to add to the drama.

'Oh dear, you poor thing!' said Maria. 'Would you like a hot blackcurrant drink?'

'Yes, please,' I said and followed her into her kitchen. It was bright and sunny, and absolutely spotless.

'Sit on one of those stools for a minute,' said Maria. I climbed up. 'What a shame,' she went on, getting out the blackcurrant cordial. 'Still, you can try again this afternoon.'

'I am never letting Dad give me another swimming lesson as long as I live,' I said. Maria was nice. You could tell her exactly what you were thinking. 'My eyes are stinging like mad!'

'That's the salt in the seawater,' said Maria. 'Hang on, I'll get you some eye drops.' She went off for a minute and came back with a tiny bottle. 'These will soothe them,' she said. 'I'll show you how to put them in. Oh, wait, I'll take my glasses off. My eyes look awfully frightening up close. Like something out of a horror film!'

She took off her glasses, and I was surprised to see that her eyes were just normal size. They looked so big through the glasses. She showed me

how to tilt my head back and drop a little bit of the liquid in the corner of each eye. Then I had to blink hard a few times. Instantly the stinging stopped.

'Oh, thank you!' I said. 'That's totally cured it.' Then I sipped my blackcurrant drink while Maria polished her glasses.

'Gosh, they're covered in grime,' she said. 'I need windscreen wipers!'

'What sort of glasses are they?' I asked.

'They're for long-sightedness,' said Maria. 'I can't see things close up. Your face is all blurred if I'm not wearing my glasses. But everything far away is as clear as anything.'

I was still a bit shivery, so Maria suggested I should go up to our room and have a hot bath. It was a great idea. I wallowed in it for ages, and the monkeys all lined up on the windowsill and watched.

'I thought Dad was my best buddy and secret partner in crime,' I told them. 'But it turns out he's a disastrous child-drowner.'

'Water!' growled Stinker. 'I hate-a da stuff! Never take us out on dat beach! Iss bad enough just being in da bathroom!'

Eventually, when my finger ends had gone all

crinkly, I got out, dried myself and put on clean shorts and a top. Then I saw a sign that Mum had put up on the dressing table: *REMEMBER SUN-SCREEN*. So I smeared a bit of that on.

When I got back out on to the beach, Sasha and Dad were building a sandcastle, and it was a terrific one.

'Wow!' I said. 'Amazing!' But secretly my heart was burning with hate, because Dad had built a sandcastle with Sasha before he'd even built one with me.

'What kept you?' asked Dad. 'I was beginning to think you'd drowned in the bath.'

'No,' I said. 'I've only nearly drowned once this morning, and it wasn't in the bath.' Dad laughed guiltily.

'Don't exaggerate, Ruby,' he said.

I saw that Sasha was smiling to herself as she smoothed down the castle walls. She was enjoying my dad and me bitching at each other. So I didn't say any more. I just sat on the towel and stared at the sea.

Lunch was a picnic on the beach. Mum had bought a huge beach parasol and insisted I sat under it. Getting it to stand up was a major challenge. Dad got into a tangle with it but luckily there were advantages to Sasha's dad being a big-headed know-all – he knew how to put parasols up.

'So,' said Dad, tucking into his crab sandwich (minus the claws and shell, by the way – it's just a pile of fishy meat, I was relieved to see.) 'How was the shopping trip, girls?'

'Oh, I bought the most wonderful pair of novelty knickers!' shrieked Deb. A crumb flew right out of her mouth and landed on the sand. 'It says *Bride of Dracula* on them! Ha ha ha ha!'

At this moment I noticed Sasha sigh slightly and fiddle with the buckle of her sandal. For a split second I felt a bit sorry for her, having such an embarrassing mum.

'More boringly, I bought a sweet little milk jug with swallows on it,' said Mum.

'And this lovely beach umbrella!' I said. 'It's like having a tent.' Then I wished I hadn't said it. I had a sudden, violent desire for a tent. I couldn't mention it right away because Mum would think her umbrella wasn't good enough. But if only I had a tent! I could pitch it on the sand or in Maria's garden, and completely get away from everybody else into my own private space.

'So how did the swimming lesson go?' asked Deb.

'Well, I nearly managed to drown her, but I think she's forgiven me,' said Dad, giving me a cheeky grin.

'Don't bank on it,' I warned him. Everybody laughed – even Paul. It was odd. Whenever I said anything sulky, it seemed to be a real success.

'We'll have another try this afternoon, eh, Ruby?' asked Dad.

How life changes things. My world was upside down. Only a few hours ago I'd planned to spend all week having swimming lessons with Dad, so I could avoid spending time with Sasha. Now I was going to have to turn the tables and be quick about it if I wanted to escape another near-death experience in the waves.

'I want to go for another walk this afternoon,' I said, turning to Sasha. 'Wanna come?'

She nodded. The grown-ups looked satisfied, and even Dad looked a tad relieved. I think he was beginning to wish he hadn't set himself this stupid project of teaching me to swim whether I liked it or not. (Originally a joke, but how horribly true it had proved to be.)

So an hour or so later, Sasha and I set off for our walk. We had five pounds each – half of our holiday money. I think the grown-ups had had a secret pact to give us exactly the same amount.

'Let's go along the sea front,' said Sasha. I agreed. There were cafes and amusement arcades and jewellery shops and places where you could buy buckets and spades and sunhats and stuff.

'I'm not going to throw my money away on junk,' said Sasha in a rather toffee-nosed way, as if she thought I was. But maybe also because of her mum buying those Dracula knickers.

'No,' I agreed. 'I don't want to buy stuff. I'd rather find something to do. Go on a train or something.'

'We couldn't go on a train without our parents,' said Sasha primly, looking shocked at my disgusting suggestion.

'I don't mean a real train,' I said. 'I mean, one of those little fun train things.'

Sasha raised her eyebrows as if she couldn't think what in the world I was on about. Then, out of the blue, we saw something totally different and amazing. It was a big board up ahead, on the pavement. And written on it in huge red letters, dripping with blood, were the words: *Chamber of Horrors*.

CHAPTER 7
Trashy and boring!

'UGH!' I YELLED. 'Horrid, horrid, horrid!' But I ran straight up and looked in at the display window. What I saw made me bite my own hands in horror and do a high-pitched squeak. There were chaps with their faces stitched across, ghosts with their heads actually right off, skulls containing mad eyeballs, women screaming with blood all down their frocks – you name it.

Sasha came up behind me and just glanced at the display in a bored way. She sighed.

'This kind of stuff is so trashy and boring!' she said. 'Come on, Ruby!' And she grabbed my arm and tried to drag me away.

Now, I'm not addicted to horror. I'm a total wuss about noises in the dark, and when my bro Joe is watching a horror film, I hide my head under the sofa cushions when the monsters are about to jump out. But I do kind of like the thrill you get when you just hear the words 'ghost train'. No way can it ever be described as boring.

And I don't like to be dragged away from something when I haven't finished looking at it.

'Let go!' I snapped, pulling my arm away.

'Oh, come on, Ruby!' said Sasha. 'This is junk, just mindless junk for idiots!'

She'd called me an idiot now. I shook her off and went back to the window. I wasn't going to be told what I could see by *her*. I pressed my nose against the glass and stared in fascination at the guy with the stitched face.

Sasha stayed on the pavement about ten metres away, looking cross, with her hands on her hips.

'Come on!' she shouted. 'Don't be so *stupid*!'

'What's the matter?' I asked tauntingly. A sudden idea had come into my head. 'You scared or something? Too scared to look?'

Sasha went bright red and scowled in a really furious way. Steam was practically coming out of her ears

'No way am I scared of that stupid rubbish!' she yelled. 'I just think it's boring, boring, boring!'

'Come here and have a look at it then, if you're not scared,' I said.

Sasha stayed right where she was.

'If you're just going to stare at that rubbish all day,' she said icily, 'I'm going back to the B&B.'

I decided to tear myself away from the display. It was only a trailer for the main Chamber of Horrors, which was a big sort of dungeon, apparently, down some steps. I knew there would be stuff down there that would be way worse.

'It's only £1.50 for kids,' I said. 'It must be really spooky down there in the dark.'

'It says if you're under twelve you have to be accompanied by an adult,' said Sasha. 'So they wouldn't have allowed us in anyway.'

'We could come back later with a grown-up,' I said.

'Ruby,' said Sasha, 'you can come back if you like, but I am definitely *not* going down there! It's just rubbish, OK? A total waste of money.'

'Scaredy cat,' I said quietly. She sighed. We walked on. I felt I'd won that round, though. I'd found a little weakness in Sasha's bossy confidence, and I filed it away in my head for future reference.

We came to a shop full of old junk. The sign said: *Antiques and Bric-a-brac.* The whole window was totally packed with wonderful things: vases, little statues, fairies made of shells and pearls hanging from threads, mugs with mysterious faces, tiny pairs of binoculars, weird little bottles that looked as if they might once have held magic spells . . .

'Let's go in,' said Sasha. It was quite dark inside. A woman with dyed blonde hair and a leopard-skin jacket was talking on a mobile phone. She gave us a disgusted look, probably because she could tell at a glance that we weren't millionaires.

Wonderful paintings hung everywhere and strange old photos of people wearing Victorian clothes and looking solemn. There were some old adverts on square sheets of tin with pictures of children blowing bubbles.

'I don't care what you say,' the leopard-skin woman was saying, 'I still think it's a disgrace. He didn't even mention it to me.'

I peered into a glass case containing lots of tiny stuffed birds. They looked alive, but they were dead. It was macabre. Sasha was exploring the far corner of the shop, where there were some old toys and clothes.

'But that's no way to behave!' said the leopard-skin woman. 'I mean, it's just totally unfair. How were we supposed to know?'

I moved on to where the books were. There were some very old-fashioned children's books there. The pictures inside were of boys all wearing short trousers and with their hair slicked back and shiny.

'*I say, Joe,*' one of the boys in the book was saying, '*I think there's a secret passage behind this wall!*' Instantly I was captivated. I wanted to be in that book. I looked at the price. It was only a pound. I decided to buy it.

'Well, I'm not having anything more to do with him,' the leopard-skin woman was saying as I approached the counter. 'He knows that. I'm never speaking to him again. Once my mind's made up, that's that.'

I hovered nearby, holding the book and getting my money out. Sasha came up to me.

'I've found something wonderful!' she whispered. I looked up. Oh my God! It was a monkey! 'I'm going to buy him,' said Sasha. 'He's only six pounds. I don't think that's bad for an antique.'

I stared at the monkey. He was carved out of wood. His head was old and shiny and he had a wonderful grin with painted teeth. His eyes were little black beads that glittered in the gloom. He was wearing a blue jacket and stripy trousers. His clothes were faded and patched. And he had a lovely tail made of leather.

I felt the most sickening feeling, as if I'd stepped into an empty lift shaft. I was dropping, dropping through space. I absolutely adored that monkey. I wanted him more than anything. Sasha knew I was famous for my monkeys, but instead

of showing him to me and asking if I wanted to buy him, she had grabbed him for herself.

'I've got to go,' said the woman on the phone. 'I've got some customers.'

'I'll take this monkey, please,' said Sasha. The woman nodded. Sasha got out her purse.

'That's six pounds. Do you want him wrapped?' asked the woman. She wasn't very friendly, considering we were children and actually buying things from her.

'No, thanks,' said Sasha. 'I'll carry him.'

I then went through the awful business of buying my book, even though I had totally lost interest in it. I couldn't bear to look at the monkey. Sasha was examining him, fascinated. Then she kissed his head.

'I'm going to call him Archibald,' she said. 'Because he is bald.'

The woman smiled, but it was a pretend smile. You could tell she was the sort of woman who hates children. We had to get out of there before she made us into a pie.

I burst back out into the sunshine and stared at the beach. It looked more beautiful than ever. Little boats were sailing out to sea. Fluffy clouds were floating in the blue. Dogs were running about and sniffing lamp posts. Everybody was just having the time of their lives, except me.

'Let's go back now,' said Sasha. 'It must be near-ly teatime.'

Although I hated the way she bossed me about all the time, now I was sunk in a kind of gloom and I couldn't care less. She had the monkey. If only I'd gone to the back of the shop before her and seen him first! If only she'd been a nice person and said, *'Hey, Ruby, here's a lovely monkey to add to your collection.'* If only.

'I suppose,' said Sasha, 'you think I should have let you buy him.'

'Oh, no!' I said, trying to sound totally surprised, as if it had never crossed my mind. 'To be honest, he's not really my sort of monkey.' *To be honest,*

I'd said, even though I'd never been *less* honest. To be honest, I was making plans even now to kidnap him and call him Jim. He was the most fascinating monkey I'd ever seen. He had what Holly calls *charisma*.

'I've got a friend who's a Goth,' I said, wanting to change the subject. 'She's called Holly Helvellyn. She's sixteen.'

'I don't like Goths,' said Sasha. 'They're weird and dirty.'

'Holly's not dirty!' I protested. 'She's clever and funny and she always helps me when I'm in a fix.' If only Holly was with me right now.

'She can't be a proper friend of yours if she's sixteen,' said Sasha. 'She must be your babysitter or something.'

'Well, she does babysit for me sometimes,' I admitted. 'But she is my friend, too, all the same. I'll send her a text and she'll text me back – just you wait and see.'

I got out my phone and texted: *HI HOL I AM ON HOL! HOL IS ACE BUT MISS YOU. LOVE RUBY X*

'No,' said Sasha. She just wouldn't give up. She was determined to put me in my place. 'I'm sorry, Ruby, but she's your *babysitter*. I've got an amazing babysitter. She's studying archaeology at Oxford University and her hair is a yard long. And her name is India de Vere.'

It seemed that, as long as I was with Sasha, I just couldn't win. I had to think of a revenge – something really humiliating. Something that would make her cry and scream and be sick in public. And make her pants fall down and make her wet herself and all her hair turn green and huge spots break out all over her face. I had to get even.

CHAPTER 8
Ssssh! Not so loud!

THAT NIGHT, at supper time, Sasha couldn't wait to show her monkey off. She brought him to the table and sat him down by her plate.

'Oh, he's wonderful!' said Mum. 'Isn't he beautiful, Ruby?' I nodded, teeth clenched.

'He's got quite a cheeky grin!' laughed Deb. 'He reminds me of somebody – I think it's the Prime Minister!' Everybody laughed. Even I grinned. I have an emergency supply of grins and I can just slip into one whether I feel like it or not. Sometimes you have to.

But really, I could hardly bear to look at the monkey. He was so unusual. I'd never seen one like him. His little black glittery eyes seemed to follow me around the room.

'I reckon it's an antique,' said Paul, turning the monkey over and looking under his clothes in a very rude way. 'Sometimes they have a mark – no, I think he's handmade.' He pulled the monkey's trousers back up and studied his face for a moment. 'Reminds me of your father,' he said to Deb.

'Oh, Paul, don't be naughty!' giggled Deb.

'These old toys can be worth a fortune,' said Paul, handing the monkey back to Sasha. 'There was a teddy bear sold at Christie's for over £100,000.'

'How ridiculous!' said Mum.

'Wish we had one!' said Deb.

'A monkey would never be as valuable as a teddy bear, of course,' said Paul. 'And this one's probably worth nothing, because it's handmade by an amateur.'

'Dad!' snapped Sasha. 'I paid six pounds for it!'

I wished they wouldn't keep calling him *it* and talking about how little he was worth. It was rude and insensitive.

'Never mind, pet,' said Deb. 'As long as you love him, that's all that matters. What are you going to call him?'

'It's a her,' said Sasha. 'I'm going to call her Ermintrude.'

'You said you were going to call him Archibald,' I said.

'I've changed my mind,' said Sasha. 'I'm going to get a dress for her. I like girl toys best.'

Of course, girls are best, in general, in the world as a whole sort of thing. I mean, that goes without saying. But anybody could see that this monkey was a boy.

'I'm going out tomorrow to look for a dress for her,' said Sasha. 'Want to come, Ruby?'

I hesitated. I was finding it hard enough to spend any time at all in Sasha's company, and now she had grabbed this divine monkey from under my nose I wasn't sure I'd be able to resist the temptation to push her under a bus. And having to watch the poor guy being forced into frocks would be absolute torture.

'I'm not sure,' I said, looking at Dad. 'Maybe I should have another swimming lesson?'

'You want to take Ruby to the indoor pool,' Paul told Dad. 'No waves there, plus it's a bit warmer at this time of year.'

'Right then, Ruby,' said Dad. 'By tomorrow afternoon you'll be swimming like a fish.'

'I hope not!' giggled Deb. 'Because fish poo in the water, don't they, and we wouldn't want Ruby to do that! Ha ha ha!' Honestly! She was so silly sometimes.

I couldn't get to sleep that night. I was trying to think of a polite way of getting out of my swimming lesson but at the same time avoiding going to the shops with Sasha. Life was so complicated on holiday. I almost wished I was back at school. Then all you have to do is get up and go there. Simple.

Another really annoying thing was that Holly hadn't answered my text. I'd hoped she would send me a lovely funny message so I could show it to Sasha and prove that Holly really was my friend. But was she? She'd ignored my text. In fact, since she'd been going out with Dom she hadn't really had time for me at all.

I was still awake when Dad came in. I could hear Mum out on the landing, talking to Deb.

'What time is it?' I asked him.

'Eleven,' said Dad. 'Haven't you been to sleep yet?'

'No,' I sighed.

'Too excited at the thought of your fabulous swimming lesson tomorrow?'

'No.' I tried not to sound too depressed at the thought of it.

'Don't worry,' said Dad. 'I won't let you drown this time.'

'Dad,' I said, 'you don't have to teach me to swim. I don't mind.'

'Of course I will!' said Dad gleefully. 'I've been looking forward to this for months. I won't rest until you're splashing about like a little frog.'

He went off into the en-suite bathroom and closed the door. Then Mum came in. I sat up and had a sip of water from the glass by my bed.

'Still awake, Ruby?' Mum smiled. 'Hasn't it been a lovely day? Did you enjoy that walk with Sasha? Isn't that a lovely monkey? I'm surprised you didn't buy it.'

'I didn't get a blinking chance!' I snapped. 'She saw him first and grabbed him and she'd paid for him before I even saw him properly.'

'Ruby!' Mum looked shocked. 'Ssssh! Not so loud!' She was afraid Sasha and her family would overhear. They were only in the next room.

'I hate her,' I said – quietly, but with all the venom I could manage. I had to tell somebody.

Mum had always supported me in the past, always understood when I was upset about something. 'She always bosses me about!' I dropped my voice to a whisper. 'She says horrible things!'

'Like what?' said Mum, sitting on the bottom of my bed and looking worried.

'Like, she said, Yasmin's name was Jasmine. And she said Holly couldn't be my friend, she must be my babysitter.'

'Ruby,' Mum smiled – it was a small, swift smile, but you could tell she wasn't taking me seriously. 'These are only little things. I expect Sasha's feeling insecure. She's just trying to impress you. Try and be a bit more tolerant. She thinks the world of you, you know.'

'Huh!' I grunted. 'That is *so* not true.'

'No, she does,' said Mum. 'It's obvious. And this buying the monkey – she was obviously copying you because you like monkeys. She thinks you're, er – cool.'

'Well, I don't like her,' I said. 'And you can't force me to.' I rolled over in the bed and stared at the wall. There were mermaids on the wallpaper and they looked a bit like Hannah at school.

'Look, Ruby, make an effort, just for me, please?' said Mum. 'I'll try and organise it so you don't have to spend very much time with Sasha, but if you can just find it in your heart to put up with her, I'd be grateful. OK?' I didn't answer. Mum sighed. 'You never know,' she went on, 'you might find you do actually like her, after all – when you get to know her properly.'

Mum likes to sweep tricky subjects under the carpet, which can be really irritating sometimes. She sighed again, got up and started getting ready for bed. I stayed looking at the mermaids.

This holiday was turning into a nightmare. There was one thing I could do, though. I could run away. Not totally, for ever, jumping ship to America or anything mega like that. I could just go missing for a day. Then they'd be sorry! They'd be so scared . . .

Moments later a brilliant idea suddenly came to me. I almost jumped out of bed and shouted 'Abracadabra!' or 'Eureka!' or another or those magic words. But I knew that for it to work properly I had to keep my plan under wraps. So I just whispered it to my monkeys under the blankets. I couldn't wait for tomorrow, so I could set it in motion.

CHAPTER 9
You won't drag me in there!

AT BREAKFAST next day, I pounced. 'Dad,' I said. 'Will you take Sasha and me to the Chamber of Horrors? You have to go in with an adult if you're under twelve.' Dad looked shifty. Mum looked faintly disgusted. Deb looked amused. Paul looked downright enthusiastic. And best of all, Sasha looked shocked and terrified. 'Or maybe somebody else could do it if you don't want to?' I went on, looking straight at her dad.

'I was thinking of birdwatching today,' said Dad, embarrassed. He didn't want to mention the time he took us to Madame Tussaud's in London. We were halfway through the Chamber of Horrors when he got a panic attack and had to run out. I'd got through it by keeping my eyes tight shut, but I had a better plan this time.

'We wanted to go this afternoon, didn't we, Sasha?' I asked cunningly. 'It looked really brilliant, didn't it?' I stared at her, daring her to disagree. She had to go along with it. If she started to make excuses, I'd be able to accuse her of being a scaredy cat and a wuss, and I'd have a major win on points that would last for the rest of the holiday.

'Or tomorrow,' she said hesitantly. OK, she'd tried to put it off, but she'd fallen straight into my trap! I was going to be able to prove that I was braver than her. Brilliant, brilliant, brilliant!

'Let's go this afternoon,' I said. 'If one of the grown-ups isn't too scared to come with us.' As my technique seemed to be working with Sasha, I decided to see if it worked on the adults as well. How brave were they?

'I'm looking forward to a peaceful day on the beach with my book,' said Mum firmly.

'You won't drag me in there!' said Deb, laughing. 'Last time I went on a ghost train I screamed so loud I wet myself! Ha ha!'

'I'll take you, no probs,' said Paul, finishing his coffee. 'I like the odd bit of horror in the afternoon. Gives me an appetite for tea.'

I laughed loudly at his joke because I felt so grateful. Dad laughed, probably also out of gratitude, because it meant he didn't have to go with us. Mum smiled a prissy little smile because secretly she thought his joke was a bit nasty. Deb roared with laughter, spit going everywhere.

Only Sasha didn't laugh. She was looking right at me. She was pale and her eyes were angry. She hated me for this. I didn't care. She deserved it for all the horrible things she'd said to me, and most of all for grabbing that adorable monkey for herself before I could catch even a glimpse of him.

He was sitting on the table beside her plate, but she'd taken his jacket and trousers off and wrapped him in a silly sparkly scarf to try and make him look more feminine. His little jet black eyes glittered at me as if to say, *'For God's sake, Ruby, rescue me from this maniac!'* I could hardly do that without actually stealing him.

Believe me, I was tempted. In the middle of the night, I'd considered eloping with him. I dreamt of creeping into Sasha's family's bedroom, lifting him gently off her pillow and vanishing with him into the night. But I don't think there are any buses at Quaymouth that take you straight to the rainforest. It's a shame, really, because if there were, they'd be really popular.

I couldn't wait for my revenge. But first I had to endure another swimming lesson with Dad. This time we went to the swimming pool. It was smelly and noisy as usual, and packed out. Dad stood shivering slightly, surrounded by six little boys all yelling. 'Jason!' 'Watch!' 'Look!' 'Dan!' 'Ben!' 'Yeaaaaaaurgh!' etc. I clung to the side and refused to budge.

The boys' mums stood around nearby, up to their waists in water and gossiping about something or other. Some of them even had babies

wearing little swimming costumes over their nappies. There didn't seem to be enough room to teach a goldfish to swim, let alone me.

'This isn't a swimming pool,' said Dad. 'It's a people soup.'

Moments later a small but perfectly-formed piece of human poo floated merrily past us. One of the babies had evidently let rip.

'Right, that's it,' said Dad. 'Out, now! I don't want to catch typhoid. Correction, I don't want *you* to catch typhoid. Don't mention this to Mum.'

We ran for the showers and stood under them for a long time. But the memory of the poo would be with me for ever.

'It wasn't people soup,' I told him as we regained

the sweet-smelling safety of the pavements, 'it was like being in a huge toilet.'

'Sorry that was so disgusting,' said Dad. 'Shall I give up trying to teach you to swim?'

'Yes, please, Dad,' I replied. What an amazing relief! No more horrid experiences involving water. Interestingly, a lot of monkeys hate water, and even the ones who have to wade through it sometimes usually carry their arms way above their heads to keep their hands dry. I reckon I'm a bit like that.

Sasha was very quiet during lunch. I could see she was tempted to tell her parents she wasn't feeling well and should maybe stay home this afternoon instead of enjoying a delightful trip to the Chamber of Horrors. Every time our eyes met, I sort of dared her to drop out. But she always looked away.

I was appalled to see the monkey was now dolled up in a pink ruffled skirt and purple top. I couldn't bear to look. This was cruelty on an unimaginable scale. If I had felt in the slightest bit guilty about the torture I was about to inflict on Sasha, her cruelty to this defenceless old monkey would have wiped it out of my mind.

We strolled along the prom: Paul, Sasha and me.

Paul was rabbiting on about great ghost trains of his youth, and how much more frightening scary stuff was back then. Sasha was silent – frozen with fear, I hoped. I noticed she was clinging to her dad's hand. A great sign!

I couldn't wait to get there. Normally I would have been a bit nervous myself. OK, I'd looked in the window and seen the display things: the man with the stitched face, the ghost with no head, etc. but I knew there would be much worse stuff inside. And it would be dark down there. I am a bit scared of the dark. And things would appear suddenly and make us jump. But I'd thought of a way of getting through it and appearing amazingly cool. All I had to do now was put my plan in action.

We arrived, Paul paid, and we went through a blood-red door hung with iron chains and festooned with ancient studs. Then we had to go down a flight of stairs. Cobwebs were hanging from the ceiling – much bigger than real cobwebs, made of kind of shiny string. And massive hairy spiders dangled above our heads. Thank goodness Yasmin wasn't here. She would have screamed the place down.

We arrived down in the basement where there

was a sign saying *DUNGEON*, surrounded by flickering red light bulbs. It was a bit tacky. I hoped it was going to be properly scary. I so wanted Sasha's hair to stand on end.

It was a huge, dark, echoing space, arranged as a series of rooms to look in – like a row of shop windows. The first one had a sign: *SWEENY TODD THE DEMON BARBER WHO MADE HIS CUSTOMERS INTO PIES*. Sasha put her arm around her dad and kind of cuddled up close to him. I stared straight in, but I didn't see anything. I'd had this brilliant idea from Maria. Maria couldn't focus on anything near because she was long-

sighted. I was going to imagine I was long-sighted now.

I could see that there was something horrid in the foreground involving blood, but I didn't focus on it. I looked at the back wall of the room, where there was a framed photograph of the Eiffel Tower.

'Blinkin' heck!' said Paul. Oh goody! The exhibit must be really horrifying if he was impressed.

'Brilliant, isn't it?' I said cheerfully, still staring at the photo on the back wall. 'Thanks so much for bringing us, Paul.' Sasha said nothing. 'What's the next one?' I said chirpily, and moved on to the next scene. The title this time was: *THE EXECUTION OF KING CHARLES I.*

I was quite tempted to look at this one, because I wanted to know if they were showing him before or after his head was cut off. But I knew I had to be firm and not look, or I might accidentally freak myself out – and I might be the one running out to be sick. So I stared at the back wall again, where somebody had painted some roofs of old-fashioned buildings against a blue sky with fluffy clouds.

'Hmmmm,' said Paul thoughtfully. 'You OK, Ruby?'

'Yeah!' I breathed, trying to sound as blood-thirsty as possible. 'I love gruesome things! What's next?'

Next was an English explorer being eaten by cannibals. I had no trouble not looking at this one, because I was sure the cannibals would be cheer-fully munching barbecued human hands and feet and stuff, and that would be so gross I'd never want to eat again. So as usual I just stared at the back wall, a painting of the jungle.

'This one's a laugh,' chuckled Paul. 'Isn't it, Sash?' He was so clearly trying to jolly her along.

I skipped merrily on to the next exhibit. 'Come and see this one!' I called. 'It's brilliant! It's called "TORTURED IN THE DUNGEON" and the next one's a vision of hell.'

Then something really scary happened. Something frantic ran past me. It was Sasha. She raced like mad towards the *EXIT* sign up at the far end. Paul looked surprised.

'Whoops,' he said. 'She's had enough. Sorry, Ruby – I think I'd better . . .' He nipped past me and rushed to the exit. I heard the door slam behind Sasha, and moments later, slam behind Paul. Now I was alone.

Ohmigawd! For an instant my insides sort of

crumpled. Now I was going to be punished for playing such a mean trick. All the ghosts would come flapping right at me and the torturers would approach my teeth with gigantic pairs of blood-stained pliers.

I suddenly saw a skull grinning at me from a corner. I jumped and gave a tiny shocked little squeak. The darkness seemed to be closing in. But I mustn't panic. I mustn't rush out looking scared to death. I must stroll out looking cool.

So I strolled as fast as possible to the exit and went out. There was a staircase up to the daylight. Phew! Several last little devils were painted on the walls, sort of waving goodbye. They looked quite sweet.

I emerged into the sunshine and looked around. There was Sasha hugging her dad, her face hidden in his jacket, sobbing violently. Victory! I had won. But as I went up to them and heard her crying, with that horrible gasping and shaking that happens when you've been really shocked, I couldn't help feeling a little tiny bit sorry for her, and just a teeny bit guilty. What on earth was the matter with me? I'd never make a gangster at this rate.

CHAPTER 10
It's Ruby's fault!

I WENT UP to Sasha and Paul, wondering if I should try to distract her with an offer to build a haunted sandcastle. But any sympathy I felt was soon swept away. Sasha turned on me and her face twisted into a horrible scowl.

'It's Ruby's fault!' she sobbed. 'She made me go!'

'Don't be daft, Sash,' said her dad. 'You said yourself you wanted to go. You can't blame Ruby.'

'Yes, I can!' screamed Sasha and she actually stamped her foot, like a toddler having a tantrum.

'She made me do it! She made me!' Paul looked at me and gave a kind of shrug.

'Sorry, Ruby,' he said. 'She's a bit upset.'

Suddenly I realised I didn't have to stay a moment longer, and in fact it would be better if I cleared off. So I just gave a kind of understanding nod, and ran off back towards the B&B. It was glorious being alone. The wind was in my hair. The sun was on my face. I had got rid of Sasha.

By the time I got back to the B&B, I was beginning to feel just a little bit guilty again. Mum and Deb were lying on the beach, reading. Mum was under the beach umbrella because she's afraid of skin cancer.

I didn't want to sit with them because Deb was Sasha's mum, and I knew she and Paul would be coming back soon and she'd probably still be raging about me. So I told Mum I was going back to the room to play with the monkeys.

I made a kind of tent under my bed by pulling the bedcover down on one side, and retreated under there with Stinker, Funky and Hewitt.

'Guys,' I said. 'It's been a really stressy afternoon, but I can report that the enemy has been totally defeated.'

'Great news!' growled Stinker. 'How'd ya do it?'

'By forcing her to look at frightening stuff,' I explained.

'Ten outa ten for genius,' said Stinker. 'I thought ya was a numbskull, but I may have been a little premature.'

Funky just lay there looking shocked, and Hewitt complained that you can't play tennis actually under the bed, but I told them we were on another expedition up the Amazon to study the howler monkeys, so this was no time for tennis really.

However, I couldn't really get into my game. I kept thinking about Sasha and how well my trick had worked, and how clever it had been to look at the back wall instead of all the gruesome stuff in front. But instead of feeling triumphant, I began to feel just a tiny bit sick. It wasn't the sort of feeling you get when you've eaten something bad. It was the sort of feeling you get when you're a bit sad.

I heard somebody go into Sasha's family's room, and then I heard them go out again. I couldn't hear who they were or what anybody said, because the voices were too muffled.

At supper it was just me, Mum and Dad. Maria had made a lovely dinner of cheese pie and salad.

'I hope your friends have a lovely time tonight,' said Maria. 'They've gone to the Golf Club for dinner, haven't they? What a treat!'

'Yes,' said Mum politely. 'But this looks like an even better treat − doesn't it, Ruby?'

I nodded. But although cheese pie is normally one of my most favourite dishes, I couldn't eat very much of it at all.

'Come on, Ruby!' said Mum. 'Eat up!'

I just moved it round my plate and wished that Joe was here. He'd wolf it all down in three enormous bites. And if Joe had been here, I'd never have had all that trouble with Sasha. She'd have been so impressed by my glamorous elder bro that she'd have made friends with me as fast as she could, instead of putting me down all the time.

'I wish Joe was here,' I said. Mum put down her knife and fork.

'Look,' she said. 'I know it hasn't worked out brilliantly between you and Sasha so far, but look on the bright side. We can do lots of things, just the three of us. We don't have to be with them all the time.'

'Don't we?' I asked. This cheered me up a bit.

'You're not the only one with relationship issues,' said Dad, winking at me.

'Brian!' whispered Mum in a warning voice. There were other families at three other tables and they might be listening. Dad just gave her a knowing grin and went on eating his cheese pie. I wondered what he meant. I saw Mum and him exchanging a very mysterious look.

'Paul's a very nice man, I think,' said Mum. 'It's just his manner.'

'And Deb's not a bad old stick,' said Dad. 'Nothing that a tranquilliser dart wouldn't fix, anyway.' I burst out laughing. It felt a bit odd. Then I realised that I hadn't laughed for absolutely ages.

'Stop it!' said Mum to Dad, suppressing a smile.

'Little ears!' This is always a reference to me hearing something I'm not supposed to. Does she think I'm stupid?

I understood the whole thing perfectly. They'd organised this holiday with Sasha's family, and it hadn't turned out as easy as they'd thought it would be. Paul was a know-it-all, Deb was embarrassing and loud, and Sasha was a control freak. I may have small ears, and possibly even a small brain, but that much was obvious.

It made me feel a bit better that the grown-ups were having problems, too. And it was nice that Sasha's family had gone out. It was lovely just being Mum and Dad and me. After supper it was still light, so we went out on the beach and built

a massive sandcastle with a moat round it, and the sea came in and filled the moat up. It was brilliant.

I didn't see Sasha again that evening, and in the morning she wasn't around either. We had breakfast with Deb.

'Paul's taken Sasha off for a boat trip today,' she said. 'They're hoping to see the seals out on the rocks down towards Seatown.' For a split second I felt jealous, because I would have liked to see the seals, too. But then right away I realised that it would have been awful, being stuck in a boat with Sasha. Somehow I knew she would be the captain and I'd end up as the galley slave.

'Dad's going birdwatching again today, Ruby,' said Mum. 'And Deb and I are going to the spa. Want to come? There's a pool and a jacuzzi and it's a ladies only morning.'

I liked the sound of that. I love jacuzzis. I packed my swimsuit, told the monkeys I'd be back at lunchtime, and arranged them on the windowsill so they could look out at the car park.

'Sorry it's not a sea view, guys,' I said.

'We hate-a da sea!' Stinker firmly. 'Give us a car any day.'

We waited for Deb out on the landing outside her room and when she came out, for a split second I saw inside their room before the door closed again. And guess what? That wonderful antique monkey had been left lying face down on the floor, still wearing the horrible Barbie clothes!

A flame of fire seemed to scorch through me. I was furious with Sasha again. I'd been feeling a bit guilty that she was so obviously avoiding me, but now I was just going to enjoy being without her. Anybody who can treat a monkey like that deserves to be taken down a peg or two.

The spa was lovely. There were several rooms all leading into one another. The walls were white and there were palms and other tropical plants everywhere. There were loads of different pools: small pools, big pools, hot pools, cold pools. There was a little wooden cabin which was the sauna. I didn't go in there because I was too young, and it was too hot so I didn't want to anyway.

Best of all, there was a massive jacuzzi. I loved it in there. The bubbles were amazing and there was a fabulous smell like lilies and roses and lavender. Mum was on one side of the jacuzzi and Deb was on the other. I kind of flopped between them, having a lovely time.

'Lie on your back a minute, Ruby,' said Deb. 'I'll hold you.' I did as she said. 'You're floating now,

love,' said Deb. I could feel her hand supporting me between my shoulder blades. 'Listen, Ruby: take a deep breath and hold it in.'

I breathed in. 'OK,' said Deb. 'Now you're like a little inflatable. The air in your lungs will keep you floating. You can't possibly sink. I've taken my hand away. See?'

I was floating! I was swimming! It was amazing! I couldn't believe it! Deb – of all people – had taught me to swim.

'But what about when I breathe out?' I yelled happily, breathing out (it's hard to yell in any other way.) Deb caught me again, laughing.

'Come on,' she said. 'Let's go in the big pool and do it again!'

CHAPTER 11

I feel amazing now

'DAD!' I YELLED when we arrived back in the evening. 'I can swim! Deb taught me! At the spa!' Dad looked surprised but pleased.

'Well done!' He gave me a hug. 'When the time comes, she can teach you to drive as well. I hate these dangerous sports.'

'Did you have a good time birdwatching?' asked Mum as she rinsed out my swimsuit in the wash basin.

'Yup,' grinned Dad. 'I saw a warbler, a gorbler, a thrasher and a flasher. And they were all lesser spotted.' I think he was just making names up. But he looked happy.

There was a lovely smell of roast beef creeping up the stairs, so we went down to dinner. I braced myself. I knew this time I would have to see Sasha again, and it was the first time I'd seen her since the Chamber of Horrors.

She and her family were already sitting at the table when we arrived. She was wearing a green dress with a pattern of leaves on it. I'm not normally interested in clothes but it reminded me of the rainforest.

'I like your dress, Sasha,' I said. She jumped slightly, as if she hadn't expected me to speak.

'Thanks,' she said. Not in a friendly way, but not in an unfriendly way either.

'How was the boat trip?' asked Mum. 'Did you see the seals?'

'Yeah. Fantastic,' said Paul, spreading a little bit of pâté on his toast. 'But I don't think Sash'll be sailing round the world single-handed when she's grown up.' He pulled a sort of teasing face. Sasha went red and stared at her plate, where a few pieces of melon were waiting.

'Didn't you enjoy it, Sasha?' asked Mum. 'Oooh, what a shame.'

'Seasick,' said Paul.

'Shush, Paul!' giggled Deb. 'Not at the table!'

'The poor little so-and-so can't help it if she's not a good sailor,' said Paul, tossing a little bit of toast into his mouth. 'I enjoyed myself, anyway.'

I peeped at Sasha. She was glaring at the table. How she must hate her dad at this moment. In fact, both her parents were way more embarrassing than mine.

'We had a fabulous time at the spa, since you're so polite as to ask!' shrieked Deb. 'I had a massage from a wonderful hunky guy who looked like Robbie Williams!'

'But the best thing was, Deb taught Ruby to

swim in the jacuzzi!' said Mum.

'I wish I'd come with you to the spa,' said Sasha to her mum. 'Can we go tomorrow?' Deb frowned.

'I'm not sure, love,' she said. 'It's a bit expensive . . .'

At that moment my mobile phone rang: the Kaiser Chiefs singing 'RUBYRUBYRUBYRUBY!' The caller ID flashed up. It was Holly!

'Holly!' I said, grinning all over my face. Mum looked cross.

'You should switch your mobile off in the dining room, Ruby!' she whispered.

'Hi, Ruby!' said Holly. 'How's the holiday?'

'The holiday's brilliant,' I said. 'And I've learnt to swim.' Mum was making angry faces at me.

'Wow! Well done you!' said Holly. 'I'll have to take you to the pool when you get back!'

'Great! But I can't talk now, sorry,' I said. 'We're having our supper.'

'Oh, sorry!' said Holly. 'I'll ring back later. I just wanted to say sorry for not replying sooner. I've been having a really tricky time with Dom. In fact, we've split up.'

'Have you?' I gasped. This was terrific news, although, of course, I couldn't say so in case she was all upset about it.

'Yep!' said Holly breezily. 'I threw him out! He was way too controlling. Just not my style at all. I feel amazing now. Totally liberated! I can do what I like. Some people you can do without, eh, Ruby?'

'You bet!' I agreed. I could feel Sasha watching me. I hoped she was impressed that my sixteen-year-old friend had rung me to confide details of her personal life.

'OK then, babe – lots of love – I'll ring you tomorrow, OK?'

'OK, talk tomorrow,' I said. I rang off and switched off my phone. 'Sorry about that,' I pulled a sorry face to everybody. 'Holly's split up with Dom,' I told Mum. Mum looked worried. 'Maybe she and Joe will get together now,' I said thought-fully.

'I wouldn't bank on it, love,' said Mum.

'It's probably best if you don't try to organise your brother's love life, Ruby!' laughed Deb. 'My brother introduced me to his best friend and look what happened!' She pulled a face at Paul and Sasha.

'I hope there'll be mustard with the roast beef,' said Dad.

'Horseradish every time, Brian!' grinned Paul. 'Are you a man or a mouse?' Typical Paul 'conversation'. Food, sport, cars, that's it.

Mind you, the roast beef was delicious. And the roast potatoes. I mashed mine up till they looked a bit like a sandcastle and surrounded them with a moat of gravy.

'Don't play with your dinner, Ruby,' said Mum. But she didn't sound really cross – just embarrassed.

Pudding was fruit salad with home-made vanilla ice cream. It was yummy beyond words.

'So, what shall we do tomorrow?' said Deb. 'Sasha, Ruby, what say we go to the safari park?'

'Good idea!' said Mum. 'There are monkeys there, Ruby – real monkeys, and they jump on the car bonnet and play with the windscreen wipers!'

Wow! I could hardly wait. What's more, I knew it meant I wouldn't be left alone with Sasha, because they'd be in their car and we'd be in ours. It would be almost as good as being on our own.

That night I got into bed early, lined up Stinker, Funky and Hewitt on my pillow and told them that tomorrow we would be seeing some real monkeys. I was halfway through explaining to them what a safari park was, when there was a tap at the door. Mum and Dad were downstairs, so I just had to call out, 'Come in!' and hope it wasn't a ghost or anything.

Sasha peeped round the door. 'Ruby . . . ?' she said. 'Sorry to disturb you. May I come in? Just for a minute?'

'Yes, but I'm in bed,' I said, panicking slightly. She was going to see my rather childish pyjamas with Winnie the Pooh on them. Sasha crept into the room towards the bed. She had one hand behind her, holding something hidden. For a split second I cringed because I thought she was going to hit me.

But when she got to the bed she just held out the marvellous antique monkey. He had got his

proper monkey clothes on. The pink Barbie frills were gone.

'I want you to have the monkey,' she said. 'I should have let you have him in the first place. I was mean. I'm sorry.'

I was so amazed I almost fell out of bed. The monkey was looking at me with his little black glittery eyes. He was just wonderful. Sasha put him right into my hand and stood back.

'You can introduce him to your other monkeys,' she said. 'What are their names?'

'I'll call him Archie,' I said. 'I think that was a good idea of yours.'

After I'd introduced Archie to the other monkeys and he'd been welcomed into their gang, Sasha said she ought to go back to bed.

'You have nice pyjamas,' I commented. They had pink elephants on. Sasha stood at the door and smiled.

'I can't wait to see those real monkeys tomorrow,' she said. 'Won't it be amazing? Goodnight, Ruby. Sweet dreams.'

'Yeah, sweet dreams,' I replied. She went out and shut the door. It had been kind of awkward, but it felt good. We weren't anything like friends yet, but I had a feeling things could only get better.

Read on for a taster of what's to come
in Ruby's next adventure . . .

Ruby Rogers

Party Pooper

Coming soon

An excerpt from:

CHAPTER 1

Ruby! Stop it!

THEY CORNERED me at break. I knew
Yasmin had something on her mind because
she hadn't been as giggly as usual. In fact, when I'd
come back from the loo in the middle of history,
I'd seen her whispering with Hannah. They were
cooking up something.

I'd tried to avoid them by imagining I was a
monkey (what else?) and swinging along the fence

at the edge of the school yard. I did a few monkey hoots, scratched my head and beat my chest like a gorilla. But a whole troupe of chimpanzees – real ones – couldn't put Yasmin off once she gets an idea in her head.

'Ruby! Listen!' She and Hannah came running up just as I reached the far corner of the fence, by the recycling bins. 'We've had a brilliant idea!'

'OOooh – oh-oh-oh-oh-oh-oh!' I cried, sticking out my lower lip and examining my fleas.

'Ruby! Stop it a minute!' Yasmin's eyes flared slightly. Her eyebrows plunged down towards her nose in a stressy frown. I couldn't ignore these warning signs. Yasmin was going to get in a strop if I didn't stop monkeying around.

'OK,' I said, transforming myself instantly into a gangster instead. 'Whassup? Give me da low-down, Big Yas.'

'I am *so* not big!' snapped Yasmin.

'Sorry,' I said. 'Diamond Lil, then.'

'Never mind all that gangster stuff!' said Yasmin. 'Just listen to our idea! We could have a sleepover on Midsummer Night! We could cele-brate with bonfires and singing and dancing and stuff to drive away the evil spirits! And we could sit up all night and watch the sun come up!'

We've been doing the Celts in history and I think Yasmin had got a bit carried away with it all. I knew it would be a mistake to argue.

'OK,' I said. 'Count me in.'

'Of course we're counting you in, Ruby!' grinned Yasmin. 'Because the sleepover's going to be at your house!'

'Yes!' said Hannah. 'I've never slept up in your tree house. Oh please, Ruby! It'll be brilliant!'

A sick feeling spread through my tum. My tree house is special. Not everybody climbs a rope ladder every time they go to bed. There's room up there for one, maybe two, but three would be too much of a squash. I didn't want Hannah up there. I knew she would flick her long hair about and make my eyes sting.

'I'd really love to,' I lied, 'but my mum will say no.'

'No, she won't!' yelled Yasmin. She was in a wild mood. Maybe an evil spirit was already egging her on. 'Your mum's lovely! She'll say yes! She won't mind!'

'Midsummer Day is at the weekend,' said Hannah. 'So everyone can have a lie in next morning. And we won't make a noise or anything.'

'So we're going to have bonfires and singing and

dancing in total silence, then?' I asked in a sarcastic voice.

'Ruby! Stop it!' snapped Yasmin. 'Anyway, it's your turn to have a sleepover! I've had a sleepover, Hannah's had a sleepover, Froggo had a sleepover at Hallowe'en – now it's your turn.'

'But you stayed at my place last week,' I argued feebly.

'That wasn't a sleepover!' hissed Yasmin. 'A sleepover is a party, right? With loads of people and games and stuff.'

I could just imagine what Mum's face would look like when I mentioned all this. She would turn to stone . . .

Ruby Rogers: Party Pooper
coming soon!